MW00947279

PERCY

The Lone Pelican

To: Owen & Alex
"Happy Reading"
Arlene Rundle

PERCY
The Lone Pelican

By Arlene Rundle

Illustrated by Jeffrey Chin

FOURTH WALL PRESS

FOURTH WALL PRESS

Text and illustrations © 2012, Arlene Rundle. All Rights Reserved.
No portion of this publication may be reproduced, shared in a retrieval system, or transmitted,
in any form or by any means, electronic, photocopying, recording, now known or hereafter devised,
without prior permission from the publisher.

Library of Congress Control Number: 2011963100

ISBN-13: 978-1468077995
ISBN-10: 1468077996

Editor: Tammy Rundle
Art direction/design: Kelly Rundle

Photo credits by page:
Kelly Rundle, p. 6, 10, 16, 36, 38
Carl Kurtz, p. 13, 28
Arthur Norris, p. 37

For bulk purchases and special sales, please contact:
Fourth Wall Press
P.O. Box 702
Moline, IL 61265

www.PelicanBook.com

For my children

Tired from a long journey, a flock of great white pelicans drifted gently on silent wings over soggy Mississippi River wetlands in Northern Illinois. As they glided down for a landing, Percy the pelican bounced off an electrical wire, brushed a tree top, and struck an old stump, injuring his left wing.

Dazed and confused, Percy rested for a few minutes. Then he waddled over to the large marsh, swam into the water and settled down for a meal.

After eating several tasty fish, Percy felt very full and a little sleepy. He scrambled onto dry land near several other pelicans and found a comfortable place to sit in the cool shade of an old tree. He gently placed his head over his throbbing, wounded wing and fell asleep.

Suddenly, Percy awoke to strange sounds near the wooded side of the swamp. A mother coyote had left two hungry pups in her den and was running along the tree line near the resting pelicans. With white wings flapping wildly, the big birds scurried back into the safety of the marsh. Percy quickly toddled in behind them. All eyes focused on the coyote as she crept near the water.

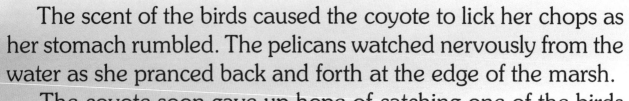

The scent of the birds caused the coyote to lick her chops as her stomach rumbled. The pelicans watched nervously from the water as she pranced back and forth at the edge of the marsh.

The coyote soon gave up hope of catching one of the birds and moved on through a farmer's field in search of food.

After a day or two of rest and feeding, the bitter cold wind of the coming winter forced the flock to continue their journey south. The pelicans paddled furiously and flapped their big black-tipped wings as they lifted themselves from the water and into the air over the mighty river. They were on their way!

All but Percy. When he tried to fly, his injured wing would not stretch out far enough. The flock flew over the wetlands where Percy sat, as though they were waiting for him to join them. After several passes, they continued their flight south leaving the wounded pelican alone!

Percy noticed a man watching him from a truck parked near the side of a gravel road. Then the man got out and waded into the water. He was coming closer and closer!

"I've got to get out of here!" squawked Percy, as he swam quickly away from the man who reached out to him. "Why is he trying to catch me?"

Unable to capture the bird, the man returned to his truck and left a trail of dust in the air as he drove away.

As night fell, Percy shivered with a chill from the cold November wind. He felt sick and weak, and his head dropped lower and lower. His wing still ached and that made it difficult for him to find food. As he drifted off to sleep, Percy thought of the flock and felt lonely for his friends.

The next day, the man returned to the marsh with a woman. Percy listened as they talked near the water's edge.

"Do you think the pelican is tangled in some fishing line?" the woman asked.

"I wondered the same thing," the man replied. "But I've seen him on land several times."

17

Percy watched as the pair drove away from the marsh. Just then, a fat fish swam near. The pelican quickly snapped his long bill into the water, sending a sharp pain through his injured wing. He missed! The fish darted safely away as Percy sat silently on the frigid water.

The next morning, the man and woman returned with a boat, a net and several more people. Soon the boat, the net and the people were in the water and moving slowly toward him! Percy flapped his one good wing and paddled wildly with his short webbed feet. Suddenly, a net dropped over his head. Percy was captured!

His heart pounded with terror as the man lifted him from the water and carried him to shore.

After looking Percy over, the man slid the trembling bird into a large metal cage and locked the door! Percy shivered with fear as he was placed in the back of the truck. Then the man draped a gray blanket over the top of the cage, leaving the frightened pelican in the dark.

Percy could feel the truck rumbling and moving beneath him. He could also hear a whooshing sound as cars passed by. He listened and swayed back and forth, and back and forth until the truck slowed and the engine stopped humming. Then he turned toward the sound of footsteps coming closer and closer. Percy's heart thumped even louder as the cage was lifted.

Soon the cover was tugged away to reveal the pelican's new shelter, a garage.

The man reached over and flipped a switch. Percy's eyes blinked at the cozy, pink glow of a heat lamp.

"It's okay," the man whispered gently, as he peered through the bars. Though Percy didn't understand the words, the kind sound of the man's voice calmed him.

Looking over the pelican's left wing, the man noticed a large cut. A few feathers were missing and the wing was swollen and infected. The man removed all of Percy's flight feathers so the bird's wing could heal.

Percy felt very uncomfortable. But before long, the swelling went down and he was able to flap and exercize his wings several times a day.

At first, Percy was afraid of the man. The bird pecked and bit at him whenever he came near. But in time, Percy began to trust his kind new friend.

Sometimes he nudged him with his powerful, yellow bill, while making happy grunting sounds. It was Percy's way of saying, "Thank you!"

Percy was feeling better and he was hungry! Local ice fishermen donated live fish for him to eat. They were placed in a child's swimming pool and Percy eagerly gobbled them up as they swam by. He ate almost three pounds of fish every day!

Using a garden hose, the man also gave Percy a shower twice a day. The warm water felt healing to Percy as he pushed his head and wings against the spray.

Percy loved to play with the man's dog. The pelican poked his bill through the cage and the dog playfully grabbed it between his paws. Sometimes the bird gently rubbed the dog's belly with his bill. The dog enjoyed the attention and often rested quietly near the cage.

One day the man looked
Percy over and said,
"Your wing is nearly healed.
Soon you'll be ready
to fly again!"

As winter turned to spring, the man gave Percy full run of his back yard. The pelican exercized his wings every day and he began to feel the urge to be free and to fly again.

He missed his friends in the flock and he longed for the feel of the Mississippi River under his belly and around his feet.

One sunny day, the man noticed that a flock of pelicans had returned to the marsh. He knew it was time for Percy to try and rejoin his friends. Once again the bird found himself taking a bumpy ride in the back of the truck.

After a short drive, the man uncovered Percy and pointed to the birds on the water. "Look who I found," he said smiling.

Percy's eyes grew big as he saw his flock bobbing in the water not far offshore!

The man gently moved the carrier to the water's edge and slowly opened the door. Percy popped his head out to get a better look and paused for a moment.

"It's okay," the man said.

Percy shot out of his cage and into the water! He swam quickly toward the pelicans who welcomed him with open wings. The big birds puffed out the pouches below their bills and shook their heads from side to side in a happy greeting.

In a few days Percy chose a mate named Kate. They gave each other loving nudges with their strong bills, while grunting happily and snacking on fish.

Later, Percy and Kate flew to an island on the river to make a nest. Kate dragged her bill across the ground as she turned around and around in a circle. Percy brought sticks for the outside of the nest and Kate added grasses to make it soft and cozy on the inside.

Soon Kate laid two eggs in the nest. The pair took turns sitting on the eggs to keep them warm. In about a month, the eggs began to crack and two baby pelicans appeared!

They were pink and without feathers at first, but in another month they were bigger and covered with white fluffy down. Percy and Kate each allowed the chicks to reach into their pouches for bits of fish. In just three short months the baby pelicans were ready to fly!

One fall morning as the flock took flight, Percy soared up into the sky with Kate and their two young ones. Drops of water sparkled like diamonds as they rained from the white wings of the rising pelicans. They were on their way to a warmer place to feed and rest during the winter months.

The man who helped Percy had been watching the young family as they grew, and he smiled through misty eyes as the great white birds disappeared from view.

He waved and whispered, "Goodbye, my friends."

Acknowledgments:

Special thanks to my son, Kelly Rundle, for his consultation throughout the entire project, and to my daughter-in-law, Tammy Rundle, for her editorial skills and project coordination. Special thanks to my daughter Mary Lindberg who is supportive of my work as a writer, and to my husband Ken Rundle who encouraged me to write this story. I greatly appreciate the advice I received from my friend Beverley Lindburg and librarian Kitty Pauwels. I am thankful to Arthur Norris, the man who rehabilitated Percy and gave me permission to tell his unique story and to use his photographs. Thanks also to Carl Kurtz for his photographs. Finally, and especially, I want to express my sincere gratitude to Jeffery Chin for his beautiful and inspired illustrations.

The real Percy the pelican!

SOURCES & ADDITIONAL READING

Getting to Know - Nature's Children: Pelicans
By Candace Saveage (1994)

Remarkable Animals Series - Pelicans
By Lynn M. Stone (1990)

Things with Wings - Pelicans: Soaring the Seas
By Frankie Stout (2008)

ONLINE

National Audubon Society - www.Audubon.org

Waterkeeper Alliance - www.Waterkeeper.org

19003714R00023

Made in the USA
Charleston, SC
02 May 2013